Marcus the Mole

Rachel McKay

Written, illustrated and published by Rachel McKay.

www.mckaybookstore.com

Marcus was a little mole,

a little mole who lived down a hole.

Down the hole there was a long tunnel.

Then another,

and another,

just like a puzzle.

Marcus spent all of his time
underground,

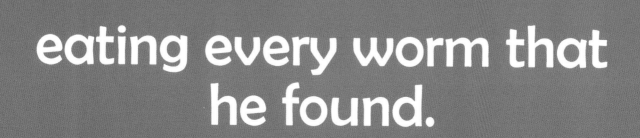

eating every worm that
he found.

Till one day, there were none there.
He could not find a worm,
not anywhere!

There were no worms cause the ground was so dry.

There just hadn't been much rain from the sky.

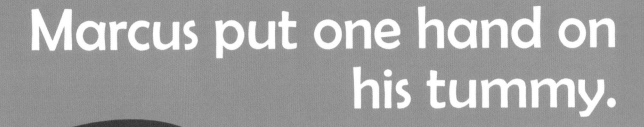

Marcus put one hand on his tummy.

"I really just need to eat something yummy!"

He crawled through the tunnels, all the way to the ground.

When he got up there, there was no one around.

"That's good" said Marcus,
"I'll just take a stroll,

to the
next
garden,
and dig a new hole."

So off little Marcus went
on his way,

looking for food, and
a new place to stay.

It wasn't long till he found a good spot.

"This is a nice little place I've got".

But just as Marcus
started to dig,

he heard something
behind him,
something big!

"Go away"
said a voice
"You can't live here."

Poor little Marcus was filled with fear!

He ran away as fast
as he could,

wishing so much that he
just had some food.

He ran,
and ran,
till he came
to a shed.

"Somewhere to live at last!"
he said.

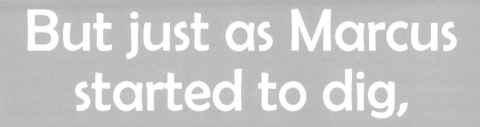

But just as Marcus
started to dig,

he heard something
behind him,
something big!

"Get out of here!" a loud
voice said.

Marcus turned around
and fled.

The poor little mole
went on his way

still looking for food,
and a new place to stay.

At last he found the perfect place.

Somewhere that Marcus could have his own space.

He looked long and hard,
but with no one around,

he started to
dig his new hole
in the ground

At last before his very eyes,
the little mole saw his prize.

There in the ground there were worms everywhere!

Worms there

and there

and there

and there.

He ate till he'd filled his tummy with food.

"Oh my!" he exclaimed, my tummy feels good!"

Marcus was a very happy mole.

So happy living in his new hole!